Walt Disney's
CLASSIC STORYBOOK

OUR HERO

DISNEY PRESS
New York • Los Angeles

CONTENTS

Printed in the United States of America

Third Edition

10 9 8 7 6 5 4 3 2

G942-9090-6-14269

Library of Congress Control Number: 2013957719

ISBN 978-1-4231-9414-9

For more Disney Press fun, visit www.disneybooks.com

Walt Disney's

Snow White
and the Seven Dwarfs

Once there was a lovely princess named Snow White. She lived in a castle with her stepmother, a beautiful but wicked queen.

The Queen was very jealous of Snow White and forced her to work as a servant. Each day, the wicked queen looked into her mirror and asked, "Magic Mirror on the wall, who is the fairest one of all?" The mirror always answered that the Queen was the fairest, which pleased her.

Meanwhile, Snow White did her chores and made friends with the courtyard doves. One day, a prince heard Snow White singing. He was enchanted by her.

The Queen saw this and became angry. Then the Magic Mirror told her that Snow White was now the fairest in the land. The Queen was furious. She ordered the Huntsman to take the princess into the forest and do away with her.

The next day, the Huntsman went for a walk with Snow White.

But she was so kind and gentle, the Huntsman couldn't bring himself to harm her. Instead, he warned the princess about the Queen's plan. He told her to run away.

Snow White didn't look back. She ran farther into the dark forest, alone and scared.

Finally, Snow White came to a clearing. She fell to the ground and began to cry. What do I do now? she wondered.

The woodland animals watched the girl. Slowly, they came out from their hiding places to comfort her.

When Snow White saw them, she smiled through her tears.

"Everything's going to be all right," she said. "But I do need a place to sleep at night."

Some birds whistled for Snow White to follow them, and they led her through the forest.

Soon Snow White and the animals came to a tiny cottage.

"Oh, it's adorable!" Snow White cried. "Just like a doll's house."

She peeked inside. It looked as if no one was home. The sink was piled high with dirty dishes, and everything was covered with dust. Snow White noticed seven tiny chairs. She decided that seven little children must live in the cottage.

"Maybe they have no mother," Snow White said to the animals.

Inside the cottage, Snow White swept the floor while the animals washed the dishes. Before long, everything shone like new.

Upstairs, Snow White found seven little beds. Each one had a name carved on it.

"Doc, Happy, Sneezy, Dopey—what funny names for children!" Snow White exclaimed. "Grumpy, Bashful, and Sleepy . . . I'm a little sleepy myself," she said, yawning.

And with that, she sank down across the little beds and fell asleep.

In the meantime, the Seven Dwarfs marched through the woods. They had been hard at work mining for diamonds all day. Now they were on their way home.

When the Dwarfs caught sight of their cottage, they stopped short. Something was very strange. Smoke curled from the chimney, and the door was open.

"Something's in there!" they cried. "What'll we do?"

They went inside to investigate and were shocked to find the place so clean. Suddenly, they heard a sound coming from upstairs.

The Seven Dwarfs tiptoed up the steps. When they reached the foot of their beds, they peeked over and saw Snow White asleep.

"Why, i-i-it's a girl!" said one of the Dwarfs.

Just then, Snow White woke up. "How do you do?" she said, surprised to see the little men staring at her.

Snow White described what had happened to her. The Dwarfs told her she could stay with them.

After dinner that night, the Dwarfs played music and danced with Snow White. She was so happy that she almost forgot about the Queen and her evil plan.

Back at the castle, the Queen did not know Snow White was still alive. "Magic Mirror on the wall, who now is the fairest one of all?" she asked.

"In the cottage of the Seven Dwarfs dwells Snow White, fairest one of all," the mirror answered.

The Queen was enraged! She came up with a plan.

The Queen hurried down to a cave beneath the palace. She used her magic to disguise herself as an old peddler woman. Then she searched for a spell to use on Snow White.

"Ah! A poison apple!" she exclaimed. "Sleeping death. One taste, and Snow White's eyes will close forever."

She climbed into a small boat and headed downstream toward the Dwarfs' cottage.

The next morning, Snow White said good-bye to the Seven
Dwarfs as they went off to work.

"Don't let anyone or anything into the house," Grumpy
warned her. Then the Dwarfs marched off to the mine.

From the shadows of the nearby trees, the Queen watched the
Dwarfs leave. Then she walked up to the cottage, still disguised.

When Snow White saw the old peddler woman, she wasn't afraid. She felt sorry for her. Then Snow White noticed the delicious-looking red apples in the woman's basket.

"Like to try one?" asked the Queen.

The birds tried to warn Snow White, but she didn't notice.

She didn't know that the peddler was really the Queen. Snow White took the poisoned apple and bit into it. Immediately, she fell to the cottage floor. The animals ran to get the Seven Dwarfs.

The Dwarfs hurried home from the mine. But they were too late. The poisoned apple had put Snow White into a deep sleep.

The Dwarfs saw the Queen running away. They chased her through the woods until she fell off a cliff and disappeared forever.

When the Dwarfs returned home, they

built a coffin of glass in the forest for Snow White. Heartbroken, they kept watch over her night and day.

After some time, the Prince who had heard Snow White singing at the castle rode by. When he saw her, he knew that she was his true love. He knelt beside her and kissed her. Snow White awoke at once. The spell was broken!

Snow White thanked the Dwarfs for all they had done to help her. She gave each of them a kiss and rode off with her prince. They lived happily ever after.

Walt Disney's
PINOCCHIO

Long ago in a little village, a wood-carver named Geppetto made a wooden puppet. It looked so much like a real boy that Geppetto gave the puppet a name—Pinocchio.

As Geppetto happily danced around his workshop with the puppet, a tiny traveler named Jiminy Cricket slipped inside. The cricket needed a warm place to sleep that night. He watched as Geppetto set the puppet down and gazed out the window at the night sky.

"I wish that my little Pinocchio might be a real boy," he said. Soon Geppetto and Jiminy Cricket fell asleep.

Before long, a
shimmering light
filled the workshop
and woke up Jiminy
Cricket. It was the
Blue Fairy. She
waved a magic wand
over Pinocchio, and
the puppet came to
life.

But he was not
yet a real boy. The Blue Fairy explained that, someday, if he was
brave, truthful, and unselfish, he would become real.

Then, knowing Pinocchio would need help, the Blue Fairy made
Jiminy Cricket the puppet's conscience. The cricket would help him
choose between right and wrong.

When Geppetto awoke, he was delighted to discover that Pinocchio could walk and talk. The old man wanted to be a good father, so he sent Pinocchio to school.

Along the way, Pinocchio met a fox named Honest John and a cat named Gideon. Pinocchio told them where he was going.

"School?!" Honest John said. "Then you haven't heard of the easy road to success. I'm speaking, my boy, of the theater!"

Honest John took Pinocchio to Stromboli, a man who owned a traveling puppet show.

That night, Pinocchio sang and danced in Stromboli's show. The crowd cheered and threw money onto the stage. But Jiminy Cricket, who was in the audience, was worried.

Later, Stromboli locked Pinocchio in a cage. "This will be your home," he said. "You will make lots of money for me!"

Pinocchio and Jiminy Cricket were very upset. How would the puppet ever escape?

Luckily, at that moment, the Blue Fairy arrived. But when she asked Pinocchio why he had missed school, he lied. His nose grew a little. Each time she asked Pinocchio a question, he lied. With each lie, his nose grew longer and longer. The Blue Fairy reminded him to always tell the truth if he wanted to become a real boy.

"Oh, I will," Pinocchio promised. The Blue Fairy fixed his nose and set him free.

On their way home, Pinocchio and Jiminy Cricket ran into Honest John again. This time, Honest John convinced Pinocchio to go to Pleasure Island. Jiminy Cricket warned Pinocchio not to go. But the puppet just wanted to have fun. He didn't think about Geppetto or that he might get worried when Pinocchio didn't come home.

On Pleasure Island, Pinocchio made friends with a boy named Lampwick. Together, they explored the island. There were rides and treats, and the boys could do anything they wanted.

But after a few days of having fun, Lampwick and Pinocchio sprouted ears and a tail. They were turning into donkeys!

When Lampwick changed completely into a donkey, Jiminy Cricket knew that he had to get Pinocchio off the island— fast! Pinocchio agreed. He was ready to go home . . . *if* they could find a way off the island.

Pinocchio and Jiminy Cricket finally escaped. But when they arrived at Geppetto's house, it was empty.

Just then, a letter fell from the sky. It explained that Geppetto had gone to look for Pinocchio.

While he was at sea, the wood-carver's ship had been swallowed by a whale named Monstro. Geppetto was living in Monstro's belly!

"I'm going to find him!" Pinocchio said to Jiminy Cricket.

Pinocchio ran until he got to the ocean, then he jumped in. Jiminy Cricket was right behind him.

The pair began to search for Geppetto.

Meanwhile, in Monstro's stomach, Geppetto was fishing. The whale had been asleep for days and had not swallowed any fish, which meant Geppetto had nothing to eat.

Still, all the wood-carver could think of was Pinocchio.

Nearby in the ocean, Pinocchio had found Monstro. As the whale awoke and swallowed a school of fish, he sucked Pinocchio into his mouth as well.

Moments later, Geppetto pulled a tuna onto the deck of his ship—with Pinocchio clutching its tail!

"Father!" Pinocchio cried.

"I'm so happy to see you!" Geppetto said, hugging his son.

"I came to save you," said Pinocchio. But Geppetto told him there was no escape. Nothing could get past Monstro's huge teeth.

Pinocchio had an idea. They would build a huge fire with lots of smoke, so the whale would sneeze and open its mouth.

As the fire grew, Pinocchio and Geppetto climbed onto a raft. Monstro's mouth opened, and the whale sneezed them into the ocean!

"We made it!" shouted Pinocchio.

Monstro was furious! He chased after the raft and smashed into it. The raft broke into pieces, knocking Geppetto out. Pinocchio grabbed his father and swam.

When Geppetto awoke, he was on the beach. But Pinocchio was nowhere in sight.

Jiminy Cricket found the wooden puppet lying among the rocks. Geppetto carried his son home in his arms, convinced he had lost Pinocchio forever.

Back in his workshop, Geppetto set Pinocchio on the bed and wept. Then the Blue Fairy appeared.

"Awake," the Blue Fairy said, waving her wand. Pinocchio had proven himself to be brave, truthful, and unselfish.

Pinocchio opened his eyes. He had become a real boy!

"Father! I'm alive!" he shouted.

"This calls for a celebration!" cried Geppetto.

He and Pinocchio danced happily. Geppetto's wish had come true at last.

Walt Disney's
The Adventures of
Mr. Toad

Tucked away among the willows, deep in the peaceful countryside, lay the homes of three friends.

In his cozy house on the river lived Mr. Water Rat, known to his friends as Ratty. Close by lived Mole, as kindly and gentle a soul as ever drew a breath.

And in the great mansion set in its own spacious park lived Toady—the madcap, reckless, extravagant, fabulous Mr. Toad.

Why, you may ask, do we call him reckless, extravagant Toad? Well, Toady, you see, was a speed demon. As a boy he went from the fastest tricycle to the fastest bicycle to the speediest boat on the river.

And even after he was quite grown up, he was still always in trouble.

It is no wonder, then, that Toad's friends were delighted when news came that Toad had reformed.

"MacBadger has had a firm talk with Toad, and he has promised to mend his ways," Ratty told Mole as they sipped their tea one afternoon.

"Splendid," said Mole, and he sighed a happy sigh. "It seems almost too good to be true!"

Alas, it *was* too good to be true! At that moment there came a knock on the door. It was the mailman with a special delivery for Mr. Water Rat.

"Come at once to Toad Hall," it said, and it was signed "A. MacBadger."

"Oh, dear," said Ratty with a shake of his head. "This means trouble."

Rat and Mole were on their way to Toad Hall when a great cloud of dust came rolling toward them. Out of the dust a voice called, "Hello, you fellows! You're the very animals I was coming to see."

It was Toad!

"We want to have a talk with you," Rat said severely. "Your reckless pranks are giving us animals a bad name. And you will soon have thrown away all your money and will have nothing to live on. You must give up your horse and cart!"

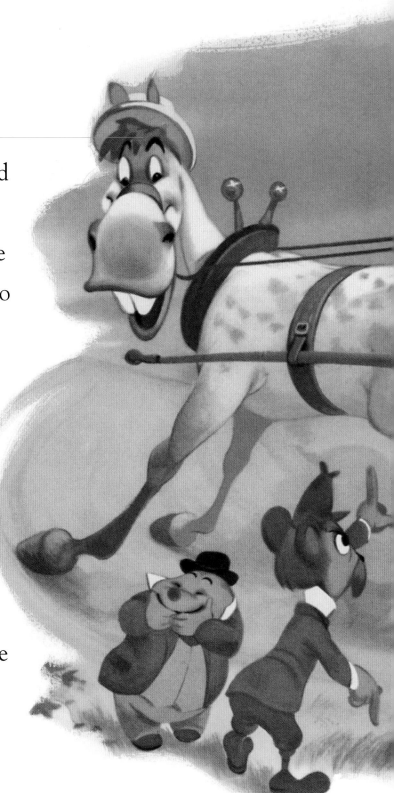

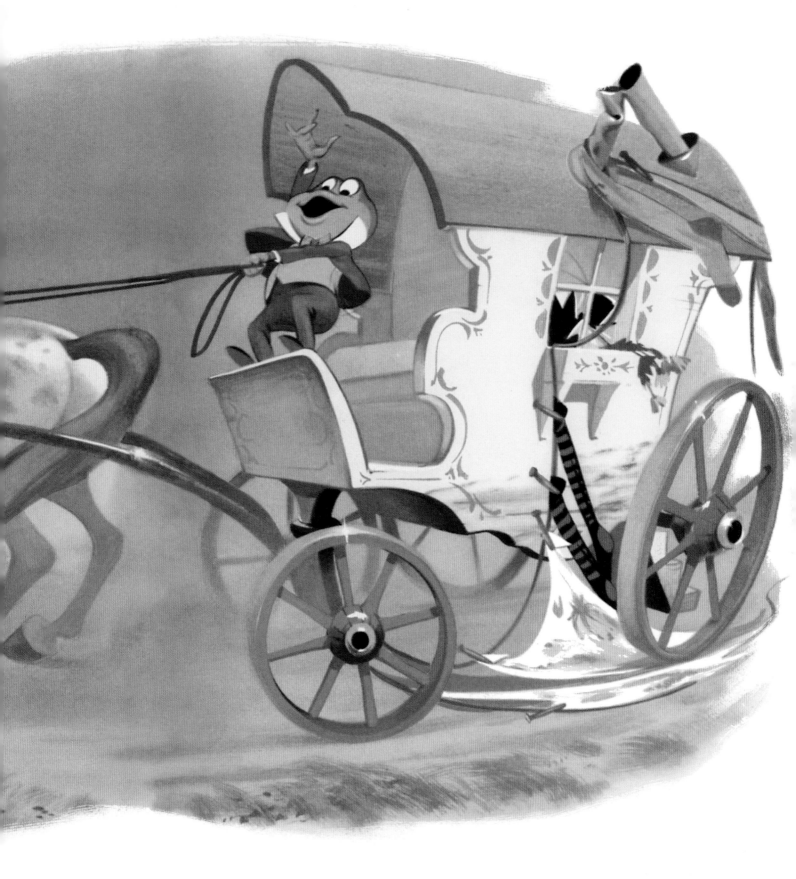

"My horse and cart! Give them up? Nonsense!" cried Toad. And he cracked his whip and started to race away, leaving behind a cloud of dust.

Suddenly a strange sound filled the air. *Honk, honk!* it went.

Toad's horse reared in fright. Over they went, horse, Toad, cart, and all, into the ditch by the side of the road.

The motorcar, for that's what had caused the accident, went chugging off out of sight.

Mole and Rat hurried over to pick up their fallen friend. "Well, Toady, this should be a lesson to you," said Ratty. "You can see that speed brings nothing but trouble. I hope you are through now with that horse and cart!"

"Horse and cart?" Toad repeated. There was a strange, faraway look in his eyes. "Oh, yes, I'm through with carts forever. I'm going to get a motorcar!"

Rat and Mole shook their heads. Then they took Toad home and put him straight to bed. Toad, you see, could not stop raving about his motorcar. And so Rat and Mole locked him in his room to keep him safe. Then they sat themselves down in the hall outside his door.

But stone walls could not keep Mr. Toad from his motorcar. He made a rope out of twisted sheets and slipped down it to the ground.

"A motorcar! A motorcar! I've got to have a motorcar!" Toad panted as he trudged down the moonlit road. "I'll have one, too, if I have to beg or borrow it!"

The next morning, Rat and Mole were surprised to see Toad in the newspaper.

TOAD ARRESTED— STEALS CAR! screamed the headlines.

"Toad!" cried his friends. "It can't be. He's safe in bed!"

Rat and Mole quickly unlocked the door and flung it open. The rope of sheets still hung out the open window. And Toad was indeed gone.

Yes, it was just as the papers said. Toad was in jail for stealing a car.

On the day of the trial, Rat and Mole sat in the courtroom, feeling sad indeed.

But not Toad. He explained to the court that he had not stolen the car at all. He had bought it from some weasels. In exchange, he had given them the deed to Toad Hall.

"The deed to Toad Hall!" The words swept through the crowded courtroom. "He traded his home for a motorcar?"

Toad's friends knew how strong his longing for speed could be, but the judge and jury did not believe him.

Toad was found guilty and sent to jail—for 99 years!

Poor Toad! For months he sat in jail, thinking everyone had forgotten him. But his mind was not idle—not Toad's! And on Christmas Eve he traded clothes with a washerwoman and made his escape.

By the time the jailer knew what had happened, Toady was on his way. Disguised as a stout little old lady, he escaped into the night.

And where did he go? Why, straight back to that quiet spot beneath the river willows, where Ratty, Mole, and MacBadger were celebrating a sad and lonely Christmas Eve.

"We've made a great mistake, lads!" MacBadger was saying when Toad appeared. "Toad *did* trade Toad Hall for a motorcar. The weasels are living there now! We must go and get the deed from them so Toady's name will be cleared!"

It was midnight when the four friends rowed silently up a secret tunnel that led from the river to Toad Hall. Up the back stairway they crept, all the way to the great hall, where the weasels were all sound asleep.

Alas, the weasels woke up just as Mole was making off with the deed to the house. The fight was on!

And, oh, what a fight it was! *Wham, slam, crash, bam!* Toad and his friends were outnumbered, but they fought like heroes and at last they won.

Toad took the deed to the court and was cleared of all charges.
Better still, he promised to give up motorcars.

"What a happy day," said Ratty when it was all settled.

"Come, lads," said MacBadger. "Let's drink a toast. To the new
year! And to the new Toad!"

Crash! The sound of falling bricks interrupted their toast. From outside the window, a voice called to them.

"Come on, you fellows!" called the voice. "This is the life! Travel, adventure, excitement! And the sky is the limit!"

The three friends ran to the window and looked out. Sure enough, there was Mr. Toad—and he was waving to them from a brand-new airplane!

Walt Disney's
Bambi

One spring morning, a deer was born in a thicket in the woods. A bird saw the tiny fawn with his mother and ran to tell the other animals. Soon rabbits and squirrels scurried toward the thicket. Robins and bluebirds settled onto the surrounding bushes.

"Wake up, Friend Owl!" a rabbit called. "It's happened! The new prince is born!"

So the owl yawned and made his way to the thicket, too. As he arrived, the baby deer stood up for the very first time.

The fawn's legs were stiff and shaky. The baby deer swayed as he walked.

"He's kinda wobbly—isn't he?" a young rabbit named Thumper said. He asked the deer's mother what the fawn's name was.

"I think I'll call him Bambi," she answered.

"Bambi," Thumper repeated. "Yep, I guess that'll do all right."

Soon the young prince grew sleepy. He lay down and took a nap.

When Bambi woke up, the chipmunks and opossums greeted him excitedly.

"Good morning, young prince," they chattered.

Bambi couldn't talk yet, but he smiled.

Soon Bambi met Thumper and his sisters. The bunnies wanted Bambi to play with them. Together they ran through the forest and hopped over branches.

Bambi tried to jump over a log, too, but he got stuck!

Bambi untangled his legs and stood up. Thumper and his sisters cheered. Then they saw something.

"Those are birds," Thumper told Bambi.

"Burr-duh," Bambi sounded out slowly. It was his first word!

Bambi was so excited that he repeated the word over and over.

When Bambi saw a yellow butterfly, he called out, "Bird!"

"No," Thumper corrected him. "That's not a bird. That's a butterfly."

Bambi followed the butterfly for a while. Then it flew into some flowers. Bambi pranced after it.

"Butterfly!" he cried at the ground.

"No," Thumper said. "That's a flower."

Thumper pushed his nose into the petals and sniffed. Bambi did the same, but he suddenly drew back. His nose had touched something warm and furry. Just then, a small black-and-white head peeked out.

"Flower!" Bambi called proudly.

The furry creature was a skunk. He blushed at Bambi.

Thumper laughed and laughed. "That's not a flower!" he exclaimed. "He's a little—"

"Oh, that's all right," the skunk said. "He can call me a flower if he wants to. I don't mind."

And so, from that day on, the skunk was known as Flower.

By midsummer, Bambi's mother decided that the fawn was ready to visit the meadow. Bambi walked to the edge of the forest. He wanted to run into the meadow, but his mother stopped him. She took a few steps forward and sniffed the air. Finally, she decided it was safe and the two went exploring.

Not long after, Bambi and his mother came to a pond. Bambi looked into the water, where he saw his reflection for the first time.

All of a sudden, Bambi saw another deer's reflection in the water.

Bambi was startled. He jumped back. Then he realized that there was a fawn standing beside him. Her name was Faline.

Bambi ran to his mother and leaned against her.

"You're not afraid, are you?" Bambi's mother asked.

Bambi shook his head. Then he looked at Faline. Faline giggled and licked his cheek.

Bambi ran away as fast as he could, but Faline chased after

him. The fawns raced all over the meadow that afternoon. Soon the two were great friends.

Over time, autumn arrived. The forest leaves turned red and orange. It rained more often, and the wind blew harder. The trees began to shed their leaves, and soon, all the branches were bare. The forest looked very different.

One cold day, Bambi woke up to find everything covered in white.

"It's snow," his mother explained. "Winter has come."

Bambi was delighted. He met Thumper at a frozen pond. The rabbit thumped his foot against the solid ice.

"Look," Thumper said, "the water's stiff."

Thumper took a running jump and slid across the pond.

Bambi tried to follow, but his legs shot out from under him. *Plop!*

He fell on the ice and knocked into Thumper, sending him spinning.

The bunny landed in a snowbank. As Thumper shook some snow off his tail, he heard snoring.

With Bambi by his side, Thumper hopped along until they came to a cave. The two friends looked inside and saw Flower. He was fast asleep.

The skunk woke up when he heard his friends calling him. Flower explained he planned to sleep all winter.

As snow began to fall, the friends said good-bye to Flower and headed for home. Bambi wondered if winter would ever end.

"It seems long, but it won't last forever," his mother said.

And she was right. Soon enough, the weather got warmer. The snow melted, flowers started to grow, and the animals woke up from their long naps.

Spring had finally returned.

Walt Disney's
THE FLYING CAR

This is the story of a boy and a professor and the most amazing old car you ever heard of.

The boy's name was Charlie. One day he was passing by the professor's house when he heard someone call his name. It was the professor. But he wasn't calling the boy. He was calling his dog, whose name was also Charlie.

Charlie was thrilled to meet a dog with his name. After that, he began visiting the professor quite often. He liked to play with Charlie the dog and teach him tricks. He also liked to watch the professor work. But most of all, he liked to polish the professor's old Model T car.

The Model T was very old and funny looking. When it chugged by, the people in town laughed at it. But what nobody knew— except the professor—was that there was something secret and very special about the car.

One night as Charlie was on his way to bed, he paused to look out the window. That was when he learned the car's secret. For up in the sky was the old Model T. It was flying!

The next morning, Charlie ran to the professor's house as fast as he could.

"Professor!" he yelled. "I saw it flying. The Model T was flying!"

"Hmmm," said the professor.

"But cars can't fly," Charlie continued. "They just can't."

The professor smiled at the boy. "I think you'd better come along with me, Charlie," he said.

The professor and Charlie got into the car and drove into the country. When they were far away from town, the professor turned a knob on the dashboard.

Suddenly, the Model T left the road and shot up into the sky.

Charlie could hardly believe his eyes. "Then it's true," he said. "The Model T really can fly! But how, Professor?"

"The secret, Charlie," said the professor, "is something I invented. Flubber. Flubber, Charlie. Flying rubber. Flubber will make anything fly. And everyone will want to have Flubber. Do you know what I'm going to do with it, Charlie, when it's ready? I'm going to give it to our president."

"Aren't you afraid somebody might steal your secret?" asked Charlie.

"Yes, I am," said the professor. "That's why I didn't tell anyone about Flubber—not even you. But now that you know, you must promise to keep the secret, Charlie."

Of course, Charlie promised.

After that, Charlie took even better care of the Model T. He polished the old car so hard it shone like a mirror. And he made sure no stranger came near it.

"Why waste your time taking care of that old wreck?" said Roy, Charlie's older brother.

"The Model T can do a lot of things the modern cars can't do," Charlie said. "Some day you'll find out."

Roy was a
member of the
school basketball
team. One snowy
Saturday, the team
left in the coach's
new station wagon.
They were going to
play a game with
Huntsville High, on
the other side of the
mountain.

Charlie's mother was worried. She didn't like Roy driving in such
bad weather. Then, around two o'clock, she got a call that the
team hadn't arrived in Huntsville.

"I just know they're stuck somewhere," she said.

Charlie hurried to the professor and told him what had happened.

"What makes it worse is that the town's tow truck has broken down," said Charlie. "What shall we do?"

"This is the time for the Model T to take over," said the professor. "Come with me."

And so Charlie and the professor jumped into the car and set off. The professor twisted the knob on the dashboard, and the Model T soared into the air.

Suddenly, Charlie gave a shout and pointed. Far below was the station wagon, stuck in a ditch.

The professor landed the Model T around a bend in the road, where the boys couldn't see it. Then he drove up to the station wagon.

"It's too bad you didn't come in a real car," said Roy. "You can't pull us out of the ditch with that old wreck."

"Oh, I think we can," the professor said calmly.

He tied a rope to the station wagon. Then he tied the other end
to the Model T and started the engine.

The old Model T lifted itself gently from the snow, and the
station wagon swung out of the ditch, as if by magic.

But nobody could be sure what was happening, for it was hard to
see in the snow. . . .

For weeks, people talked of nothing else but how the Model T had saved the station wagon.

Then, at last, the day came that the professor had finished his work on Flubber. As the town watched, the professor flew his car off to give his wonderful invention to the president.

"Wow," Roy said. "That Model T is some car!"

Walt Disney's
Cinderella

Once upon a time, there was a kind gentleman. He lived in a mansion with his lovely daughter. He gave her everything money could buy. But the child didn't have a mother or any friends her own age. So the gentleman married a woman named Lady Tremaine, who had two daughters, Anastasia and Drizella. He hoped this would make his little girl happy.

Soon after, the gentleman died, and Lady Tremaine revealed just how jealous she was of his daughter. The cruel woman forced her stepdaughter to work as a servant. She sent the girl to sleep in the musty attic and called her Cinderella.

Cinderella was never sad, though. As she grew up, she made friends with the birds who nested nearby and the mice who lived in the attic.

The animals thought Cinderella was the sweetest and most beautiful girl in the world. Every morning, the mice and birds woke Cinderella from her dreams so that she could begin her long day of chores. Cinderella started by feeding Lady Tremaine's nasty cat, Lucifer. Then she fed the barnyard animals and the mice.

Finally, she got breakfast trays ready for her stepmother and stepsisters.

"Pick up the laundry and get on with your duties," Lady Tremaine would often say when Cinderella arrived with breakfast.

"Yes, Stepmother," Cinderella always answered politely.

One day, Lady Tremaine received an announcement from the King. There was to be a ball at the palace that night in honor of the Prince. By royal command, all eligible maidens were to attend.

"Why, that means I can go, too!" Cinderella exclaimed.

Lady Tremaine looked at her coldly. "I see no reason why you can't go," she said. "If you get all your work done."

Cinderella worked hard all day long. But there were just too many chores. Poor Cinderella returned to her attic. She hadn't had any time to find a ball gown.

Just then, the mice and birds surprised Cinderella. They had fixed up a gown for her to wear!

Cinderella hurried down the stairs. "Wait! Please!" she called.
Hearing Cinderella's voice, Lady Tremaine, Anastasia, and

Drizella turned
and stared at her
lovely gown.

In a rage, her
stepsisters pulled
and ripped at
Cinderella's dress
until it was in
tatters.

Cinderella ran
to the backyard
and cried. "There's nothing left to believe in," she said.

"Oh, now, you really don't mean that," a gentle voice said. "If
you'd lost all your faith, I couldn't be here. And here I am."

Cinderella looked up and saw a woman with a magic wand standing in front of her. It was her fairy godmother!

With a wave of her wand, the woman transformed a pumpkin into a coach, four mice into white horses, a horse into a coachman, and the barnyard dog into a footman.

Then the Fairy Godmother noticed Cinderella's ripped clothing. She made her a beautiful gown and tiny glass slippers. She warned Cinderella that the magic would last only until midnight.

By the time Cinderella's coach arrived at the palace, the ball had already begun.

The King stood with the Grand Duke on the balcony above the dance floor. He hoped that his son would fall in love with a maiden that night.

Just then, Cinderella entered the ballroom. The King and the Grand Duke watched as the Prince walked over to her.

The King beckoned to his musicians to strike up a waltz. The Prince and Cinderella whirled across the floor.

All evening, the Prince stayed by Cinderella's side. Cinderella had such a wonderful time that she forgot about her fairy godmother's warning. All of a sudden, the clock in the palace tower began to strike midnight. *Bong! Bong!*

"Oh!" Cinderella said good-bye to the Prince and ran toward the palace door. As she ran, one of her glass slippers flew off. But Cinderella couldn't stop. She had to get home before the magic wore off.

Cinderella leaped into the coach and raced for home. As she rounded the first corner, the clock struck twelve. The spell was broken, and Cinderella and her friends changed back to the way they'd looked before the ball.

"Cinderelly, your slipper!" the mice called.

She looked down. Sure enough, one glass slipper remained on the pavement.

"Thank you so much for everything," Cinderella said in a hushed voice. She knew her fairy godmother could hear her.

Back at the palace, the King was upset that the girl had run away. All she had left behind was one of her tiny slippers.

The King instructed the Grand Duke to find the girl whose foot fit the slipper.

The next morning, when Cinderella heard that the Grand Duke was coming with the slipper, she dropped a breakfast tray in shock.

Lady Tremaine saw the dreamy look in Cinderella's eyes. She suspected that Cinderella was the girl whom the Prince had fallen in love with.

When Cinderella went into her bedroom, her wicked stepmother locked her inside.

The Grand Duke reached Cinderella's home and held the small slipper up to Anastasia's huge foot. But try as she might, the girl could not make the shoe fit.

Meanwhile, the mice crept toward Lady Tremaine's chair. They were determined to free Cinderella. The mouse at the front dropped down into her coat pocket and grabbed the key to Cinderella's room! Then the mice scurried off to the attic and freed Cinderella.

When Cinderella got downstairs, she saw that the Grand Duke was leaving.

"Your Grace!" she called out. "Please wait! May I try it on?"

The footman carried the shoe toward the girl,

but Lady Tremaine tripped him and the slipper fell! *Crash!* It shattered into a thousand pieces.

Cinderella was not upset. "You see, I have the other slipper," she said.

Lady Tremaine was horrified, but the Grand Duke was very happy. The footman tried the slipper on Cinderella. It fit perfectly!

Soon Cinderella traveled to the palace. The Prince was overjoyed to see her again. The King was quite delighted, too. In fact, the entire kingdom was thrilled, for Cinderella won the heart of everyone she met.

Cinderella and the Prince were married, and she became a princess. The royal couple lived happily ever after.

Walt Disney's
THE UGLY DUCKLING

In the heart of the beautiful countryside lived a mother duck. Her nest was in the loveliest spot under a big, shady tree. She longed to stretch her legs and go for a swim in the warm summer sun. But instead she sat patiently, waiting for her five eggs to hatch.

After many long and quiet days, Mother Duck heard a pecking sound. Could it be time?

Mother Duck hopped off her nest to peek at the eggs. One wiggled. Another wobbled. The pecking sounds got louder and louder.

Crack-crack-crack-crack! Out popped one . . . two . . . three . . . *four* fuzzy ducklings!

The downy youngsters scrambled out of their shells as quickly as their webbed feet could waddle.

"Follow me," Mother Duck smiled. "We'll go for a refreshing swim in the lake."

But before she could lead her ducklings to the water, Mother Duck remembered the fifth egg.

"Oh, dear!" she cried. "The biggest egg of all still hasn't hatched. Oh, well, I sat this long. I might as well sit a bit longer." And so, Mother Duck settled back down on the biggest egg.

Finally, after a very long time, the big egg began to wiggle and wobble. Mother Duck and her precious ducklings gathered around the nest to watch. At last, *crrrrack!* The new hatchling broke out of his shell!

Instead of being sunshiny yellow, the new duckling was a dull gray. And he was awfully big.

"Honk! Honk!" he greeted his new family.

But his brothers and sisters weren't so friendly.

"You're *ugly!*" quacked the ducklings.

"You must be a turkey," Mother Duck said. "All my other children are the spitting image of their father." Then Mother Duck turned her back on the big hatchling and quacked to the others. "Come along, children, we've waited long enough to go for a swim."
The Ugly Duckling wanted to swim, too. He followed the others to the lake and floated easily on the surface.

The cool water felt so refreshing on his big, floppy feet!

"Look, Mom! I can swim, too!" he called. But Mother Duck and the ducklings swam away and pretended not to notice him.

Heartbroken, the Ugly Duckling swam to a quiet spot among the marshy reeds. There, hidden from the rest of the world, the poor duckling dropped his head and cried.

As the Ugly Duckling looked at the ripples his tears made in the water, he saw a horrible sight. It was his own reflection.

"I *am* ugly!" he cried. "No wonder no one wants to be near me!"

The Ugly Duckling decided to run far away where no one would be bothered by his ugliness. He waddled through fields and glens, deep into the forest. Finally, he came upon a clearing where he saw a nest of young birds chirping happily away.

The Ugly Duckling climbed into the tree. "Come play with us," the baby birds said. "Mother is returning soon with food. She'll be happy to have you in our nest."

And so the Ugly Duckling played with his new brothers and sisters and waited patiently for Mother Bird.

Soon Mother Bird came home with a fat, juicy worm in her mouth. The Ugly Duckling had forgotten how hungry he was and snapped the worm right out of Mother Bird's beak and swallowed it whole.

"*Squawk, squawk, squawk!*" scolded Mother Bird. "Shame on you, you big ugly thing! How dare you take food away from my babies!"

And she shooed him out of her nest and far away from her children.

The Ugly Duckling wandered for many lonely hours until he came to a large pond. There, floating among the reeds, he saw the biggest, friendliest-looking duck he had ever seen.

"Perhaps he won't mind that I'm so ugly," he said hopefully.

The Ugly Duckling snuggled close to his newfound friend. He was so overcome with happiness, he didn't even notice that the mallard wasn't a duck at all. He was nothing more than painted wood.

The Ugly Duckling nudged the smiling decoy. "Let's play!" he honked.

The wooden duck bobbed his head up and down and up and down.

"At last! Someone wants to play with me!" cried the Ugly Duckling. Excited, he climbed onto the big duck's back and jumped into the water. *Splash!* What fun!

He continued to splash and play, filling the pond with waves. The decoy bobbed back and forth until . . . *BONK!* Its big, wooden bill hit the Ugly Duckling smack-dab in the middle of his forehead.

The Ugly Duckling paddled to safety as quickly as he could. Then he flopped onto a log and cried his little heart out.

Suddenly, he heard a *honk-honk-honking* all around him. He looked up and saw the most wonderful sight of all—a flock of magnificent young birds. He thought they were the loveliest creatures he'd ever seen.

If only he could be half as lovely!

The Ugly Duckling was so elated to have company that he dove all the way to the bottom of the pond. But when he popped up at the surface, he found himself alone again.

The other birds were paddling away, *honk-honk-honking* in the distance.

Why should I think that they would want to play with me? the Ugly Duckling thought gloomily.

Just when he thought he would be alone and miserable forever, something amazing happened! The beautiful birds returned. And with them swam the most glorious bird in the world.

"Look, Mother!" honked the happy swans. "We've found a new brother!"

The Ugly Duckling couldn't believe his eyes or his ears.

"You're home now, little one," said the mother swan as she cradled the Ugly Duckling under her snowy-white wing. "You are a fine young swan."

From the shore, Mother Duck and her ducklings watched the graceful swan welcome the Ugly Duckling into her family.

As he swam away with his new family, the Ugly Duckling ruffled his feathers and held his head up high. Never before had he felt so much love in his heart.

Walt Disney's
ALICE
in
WONDERLAND

One beautiful day, a girl named Alice took a walk outside with her older sister. When they reached a riverbank, Alice climbed to a high tree branch and settled into a comfortable spot. Her sister sat on the ground and started reading out loud from a history book.

It was warm outside, and Alice didn't feel like paying attention. Instead, she played with her cat, Dinah. Soon she began to daydream. Alice imagined a world where animals and flowers could talk.

Just then, Alice looked up and spotted a rabbit who was carrying a pocket watch!

"I'm late!" the White Rabbit called as he ran by. Alice was curious. She climbed down from the tree and tried to catch up.

Alice followed the rabbit into a hole in the ground. Suddenly, she began to fall down a long tunnel. She landed in time to see the White Rabbit race through a tiny door.

Alice tried to go after him, but she was too big. She shut the door.

"Try the bottle," someone suggested.

Alice looked around, startled. It was the Doorknob!

Suddenly, a bottle appeared on a nearby table. The label on it read DRINK ME, so Alice tried a little.

All at once, Alice began to shrink. Soon she was so small that she could stand on the table leg. She tried opening the door, but it was locked. And the key was on the tabletop far above her.

Then the Doorknob told Alice to try a cookie that was labeled EAT ME. As Alice ate it, she grew larger. She became her normal

height and then kept on getting bigger. By the time she stopped growing, Alice was enormous.

Alice was frustrated. She cried, and her giant tears started a flood. For the second time, the Doorknob suggested that Alice drink from the bottle. This time she became so tiny that she fit *inside* the bottle. The bottle—with Alice—floated through the keyhole.

On the other side, she met twins named Tweedledee and Tweedledum. Alice explained that she was following the White Rabbit. But the twins didn't care. They began to tell her a story.

Alice wanted to be polite, so she listened. But when the twins finished their tale, they just kept talking. Finally, Alice decided to leave.

At last, Alice spotted the White Rabbit in his yard. He was worried because he couldn't find his white gloves.

"I'm late!" he told Alice again.

Alice offered to help, and the two began to search the house. Inside, Alice took a bite of some food labeled EAT ME. She immediately grew into a giant. Her long arms and legs crashed through the cottage's windows and doors.

The White Rabbit panicked and ran to get some help.

Meanwhile, Alice searched for something that would make her shrink again. She plucked a carrot out of the White Rabbit's garden and took a bite. All at once, she shrank to a tiny size.

The White Rabbit returned and, thinking Alice gone, continued on his way. Alice tried to follow, but she was too slow.

Soon Alice found herself in an unusual garden. She was delighted by all of the strange things that surrounded her. Odd bugs, including bread-and-butterflies and a rocking-horsefly, flew through the air. Most of the flowers were taller than she was, and they could *speak!*

But the flowers thought Alice was a weed, and they told her to leave their garden.

Next Alice came to a caterpillar sitting on a mushroom. The Caterpillar told Alice that eating some of the mushroom would help her.

"One side will make you grow taller. And the other side will make you grow shorter," he said.

"Which is which?" Alice wondered, breaking off a piece from each side.

Alice took a bite of one side and shot up taller than the trees. She even scared a bird that was nesting on a high branch.

Soon Alice began to understand how she could use the mushroom to control her height. She took small bites of the other side of the mushroom. With each bite, she shrunk a bit more until she reached her regular size.

As Alice wandered back through the forest, she saw a cat appear in a tree. He introduced himself as the Cheshire Cat and suggested that she speak with the Mad Hatter.

Alice didn't like the idea of meeting someone mad, but perhaps the Hatter would know where she could find the White Rabbit.

Alice continued through the forest until she reached a strange tea party. The Mad Hatter and March Hare were celebrating their unbirthdays. They invited Alice to tea.

When the Mad Hatter and the March Hare discovered that it was Alice's unbirthday, too, they gave her a cake.

As Alice blew out the candles, the cake shot into the sky like a rocket. A dormouse holding a tiny umbrella floated down and

landed in a teapot. Alice had never seen such nonsense.

Alice was just about to leave the party when, to her surprise, the White Rabbit ran by. He looked at his watch and cried, "I'm late!"

The White Rabbit ran off and Alice ran after him.

Alice soon lost sight of the White Rabbit. As she continued searching for him, she found herself in a fancy garden. She watched as some playing cards painted white roses red.

Suddenly, the White Rabbit ran into the garden. He was there to announce the Queen of Hearts.

When the Queen saw that some of the roses were still white, she was furious.

"Off with their heads!" she shouted, pointing at the poor playing cards.

Just then, the Queen of Hearts spotted Alice. She challenged the girl to an odd game of croquet, using hedgehogs as balls and flamingos as mallets. The Queen began to win but only because she cheated.

Suddenly, the Cheshire Cat reappeared. Alice spoke to the cat, but he hid himself from the Queen of Hearts. The Queen thought Alice was teasing her and cried, "Off with her head!"

Alice started to run. But the Queen and her guards chased after her.

Alice ran until she reached the talking doorknob once more.

"I simply must get out," she pleaded.

"But you *are* outside," the Doorknob said. "See for yourself."

Alice peered through the keyhole and saw herself sitting in the tree with her cat, Dinah. She realized that she was in a dream, and she wished that she would wake up.

Sure enough, when Alice awoke, she was back in the tree. It was a lovely afternoon and there wasn't a bit of nonsense. That was just fine with Alice.

Walt Disney's
PLUTO PUP
GOES TO SEA

Mickey and Pluto Pup were standing beside an ocean liner, looking up at the deck.

Mickey pointed at the ship. "Why can't you be a hero like that ship's dog?" he asked Pluto Pup.

On the deck lay a huge dog, staring proudly out to sea.

"There was a story in the paper about all the lives he's saved," said Mickey.

Pluto looked at the dog. If all it took to be a hero was lying on a deck and staring out to sea, he was willing to give it a try. So the next time he and Mickey passed a gangplank, up Pluto went.

When Mickey noticed that Pluto was gone, he whistled and called for him. He looked behind crates and barrels and in coils of rope, but he could not find Pluto Pup anywhere.

High above, on the deck of a sleek white yacht, Pluto was sitting all alone, looking proud and gazing out to sea. Surely now he would be a hero!

Soon the boat left the harbor for the open sea. Not long after, a tough-looking sailor found Pluto Pup and led him belowdecks.

"Too bad he isn't a smarter mutt," said the second mate to the first. "We could use a smart watchdog for the captain's jewels."

"Shh!" the first mate said. "No one must know about those jewels!"

But it was too late. The tough-looking sailor who had found Pluto had overheard the second mate.

"Them jewels will line my pockets soon, and I'll jump ship at the very first port, or my name's not Pegleg Pete!" he said.

The next day as Pluto Pup explored the ship, his nose led him to the galley, where the ship's cat lived with the cook.

Pluto sniffed at the cat, who arched her back and hissed at him. Startled, Pluto Pup raced back to the deck. But the cat was close behind him.

Suddenly, the ship lurched. The cat slid under the rail and down into the sea!

Pluto edged closer to the railing for a better look—and fell in right behind her!

The sailors soon rescued the animals. They did not know what had really happened. They thought Pluto had jumped in to save the cat. They called him a hero and fussed over him. They even moved his bed to the captain's cabin.

"He's just the dog we need to guard the captain's jewels," they said.

But Pluto did not like being shut in the cabin. He howled so loudly that the captain shouted for the sailors.

"Take that mutt away. I'd rather be guarded *from* him than *by* him!" he cried.

Pluto happily went back to the deck, where he kept a sharp eye out for anyone about to fall overboard.

But while Pluto was watching for trouble on the deck, something bad was happening belowdecks. Pegleg Pete had slipped into the captain's cabin. He hit the captain on the head and stole his jewels!

With the jewels safely stowed in a small leather pouch, Pegleg Pete signaled to his friends onshore.

When a small light answered, he kicked off his shoe and dove over the rail into the water below.

Splash! He landed and started to swim, but Pluto had heard that splash. He thought Pete was in trouble and jumped into the water to save him.

Hearing Pluto Pup's bark, the sailors turned on the searchlight and pulled the two out of the water.

"I saw the dear mutt slide in," Pete claimed, "so I jumped in to save him."

"Is that so?" said the first mate. "Then why is your shoe still on the deck?"

"Come to think of it, where's the captain?" the second mate cried. And he ran to the cabin to see.

161

Pegleg Pete knew he was caught. "Let me go!" he cried, and he ran for the rail.

But Pluto did not want another bath in that cold water. He jumped for Pete's trousers and hung on!

Soon the second mate returned with the captain.

"Put Pete in the brig," the captain said. "And get this pup a medal!"

A few days later, the yacht returned to the docks. Pluto was sitting proudly up on deck wearing the biggest, shiniest medal he had ever seen.

Mickey was wandering down by the docks, as he did every lonely day, looking for his lost pup, when the yacht came into port.

"Arf!" cried Pluto, when he spied Mickey Mouse.

"Pluto!" cried Mickey. "Where have you been?"

The sailors told Mickey the whole proud tale.

"Now that you're a hero, I guess you won't want to come back home," Mickey said.

The happy pup gnawed his medal off and laid it at Mickey's feet. He still thought the finest thing of all was to be Mickey Mouse's dog!

Walt Disney's
Peter Pan

Mr. and Mrs. Darling lived on a quiet street in London with their children, Wendy, Michael, and John, and their dog, Nana.

Every night, Wendy told her brothers stories about a magical boy named Peter Pan and about Never Land, the island where he lived.

But Mr. Darling did not like her stories. He thought his daughter was too old to believe in Never Land.

Finally, one night he said, "Young lady, this is your last night in the nursery."

Later that night, after Mr. and Mrs. Darling had left for the evening, Peter Pan and his fairy friend Tinker Bell appeared. They were looking for Peter's lost shadow.

Tinker Bell soon found the shadow, but the boy needed someone to reattach it.

Wendy had woken up and offered to help. As she sewed, she told Peter it was her last night in the nursery.

"No, I won't have it!" Peter exclaimed. He didn't want her to grow up. "Come on to Never Land!"

Wendy agreed as long as Michael and John could go, too. And so, with the help of some pixie dust from Tinker Bell, Peter Pan taught them all to fly.

Back in Never Land, Captain Hook was looking for Peter Pan. Just then, a pirate yelled, "Peter Pan, ahoy!"

Captain Hook spied Peter and the Darling children sitting on a cloud overhead. "We'll get him this time!" Captain Hook cried. "Man the long cannon!"

In the sky, the children were admiring the view of Never Land. Suddenly, a cannonball shot through the cloud.

"Quick, Tink! Take Wendy and the boys to the island. I'll stay here and draw Hook's fire," Peter said.

Tinker Bell and the children quickly flew to Peter's hideout.
Not long after, Peter joined them. He offered to take Wendy to
Mermaid Lagoon while John and Michael explored the jungle with
Peter's Lost Boys.

Peter and Wendy had just reached the lagoon when they caught
sight of Captain Hook and his first mate, Mr. Smee. The pirates
had taken Tiger Lily, the Indian Chief's daughter, prisoner.

Peter followed Captain Hook to Skull Island.

"Now, my dear princess, you tell me the hiding place of Peter Pan, and I shall set you free," Captain Hook said.

Tiger Lily refused, so Mr. Smee set her on a rock in the water and waited for the tide to rise.

Just then, Peter jumped out from behind another rock and began to fight Captain Hook. When they reached a cliff, Peter jumped, and Captain Hook tumbled down into the water.

Peter quickly rescued Tiger Lily.

While Peter brought Tiger Lily home, Mr. Smee captured Tinker Bell.

"Beggin' your pardon, Miss Bell, but Captain Hook would like a talk with you," he said.

Captain Hook told Tinker Bell that he was going to sail away from Never Land. He offered to kidnap Wendy and take her with them if Tinker Bell would tell him the location of Peter's hideout.

Tinker Bell liked Captain Hook's plan, for Peter seemed to have forgotten about her since Wendy had arrived, and happily marked the spot on the map.

Inside Peter's hideout, Wendy told the boy that she thought it was time to go home. Angry that she wanted to leave, Peter turned his back on the girl.

When Wendy and the other children climbed out of the hideout, Captain Hook and his pirates were waiting for them. They captured the children and tied them up.

Then Captain Hook pulled out a gift-wrapped package with a tag that read "From Wendy." Inside was a bomb! Captain Hook lowered the gift into Peter's hideout and left.

Tinker Bell hadn't known that Captain Hook was going to harm Peter. When she realized the truth, she sped toward Peter's hideout and grabbed the bomb away from Peter before it could explode.

On board the pirate ship, Captain Hook gave the children a choice: become pirates or walk the plank.

Refusing to be a pirate, Wendy said good-bye to the boys and bravely walked out onto the plank.

Then she stepped off the edge and disappeared. The pirates listened for a splash, but there wasn't one.

Peter had arrived and caught Wendy.

"This time, you have gone too far!" Peter yelled. He placed Wendy on the deck, and then he and Hook began to duel.

While they battled, Tinker Bell freed the Lost Boys, who fought the pirate crew. At last, Peter and the boys had sent every last pirate, including Captain Hook, overboard.

Peter took command of the ship. "We're casting off!" he cried.

"Where are we sailing?" Wendy asked.

"To London," Peter said.

Tinker Bell sprinkled pixie dust over the ship, and it rose into the air.

At last, the ship reached the Darlings' home. The Darling children climbed through the nursery window and waved good-bye to Peter and the Lost Boys.

Wendy knew now that she was ready to grow up. But she also knew that no matter how old she got, she would never forget her amazing adventure with Peter Pan!

Walt Disney's
THREE LITTLE PIGS

Once upon a time there were three little pigs who went out into the big world to build their homes and seek their fortunes.

The first little pig did not like to work at all. He quickly built himself a house of straw. Then off he danced down the road to see how his brothers were getting along.

The second little pig was building himself a house, too. He did not like to work any more than his brother, so he had decided to build a quick and easy house of sticks.

Soon it was finished. Now the second little pig was free to do what he liked. And what he liked to do was to play his fiddle and dance.

The second little pig danced and sang:

> *"I built my house of sticks,*
> *I built my house of twigs.*
> *With a hey diddle-diddle*
> *I play on my fiddle,*
> *And dance all kinds of jigs."*

Soon he came upon the first little pig, who began to dance with him. Playing their flute and their fiddle, the two little pigs danced down the road together to see how their brother was getting along.

The third little pig was a serious pig. He was building a house, too, but he was building *his* out of bricks. He did not mind hard work, and he wanted a strong little house, for he knew that in the woods nearby there lived a big bad wolf who liked nothing better than to catch little pigs and eat them up!

"Ha ha ha!" laughed the first little pig when he saw his brother hard at work.

"Ho ho ho!" laughed the second little pig. "Come down and play with us!" he called.

But the busy little pig did not pause. *Slap, slosh, slap!* went the bricks and mortar.

"You can laugh and dance and sing," their busy brother called after them, "but I'll be safe and you'll be sorry when the wolf comes to the door!"

"Ha ha ha! Ho ho ho!" laughed the two little pigs again, and they disappeared into the woods.

But as the first pig reached his door, out of the woods popped the big bad wolf! The little pig squealed with fright and slammed the door.

"Little pig, little pig, let me come in!" cried the wolf.

The little pig knew better than to open his door for a wolf. "Not by the hair of my chinny-chin-chin!" he said.

"Then I'll huff and I'll puff and I'll blow your house in!" roared the wolf. And he blew the little straw house all to pieces!

Away raced the little pig to his brother's house of sticks. But no sooner was he in the door than the big bad wolf appeared!

"I'll fool those little pigs," said the big bad wolf when the pigs would not let him inside. And so he left the little pig's house and hid behind a tree.

Soon the door opened and the two little pigs peeked out. There was no wolf in sight.

"Ha ha ha! Ho ho ho!" laughed the two little pigs. "We fooled him."

Then they went back inside and danced around the room.

Soon there came another knock at

the door. It was the big bad wolf again, but he had covered himself with a sheepskin, and was curled up in a big basket, looking like a little lamb.

THREE LITTLE PIGS

"Who's there?" called the second little pig.

"I'm a poor little sheep with no place to sleep. Please open the door and let me in," said the big bad wolf in a sweet little voice.

The little pig peeked through a crack in the door. He could see the wolf's big black paws and sharp fangs.

"Not by the hair of my chinny-chin-chin!" he cried.

"You can't fool us with that sheepskin!" said the first little pig.

193

"Then I'll huff, and I'll puff, and I'll blow your house in!" cried the angry old wolf.

So he huffed and he PUFFED and he *puffed* and he HUFFED, and he blew the little twig house all to pieces!

Away raced the two little pigs, straight to the third little pig's house of bricks.

"Don't worry," said the third little pig to his two frightened little brothers. "You are safe here."

Soon the three little pigs were all singing happily. This made the big bad wolf perfectly furious!

The big bad wolf huffed and he PUFFED, and he *puffed* and he HUFFED, but he could not blow down that little house of bricks!

At last he thought of the chimney! Up he climbed, quietly. Then with a snarl, down he jumped—right into a kettle of boiling water! With a yelp of pain he sprang straight up the chimney again and raced away into the woods.

The three little pigs never saw him again and spent their time in the strong little brick house singing and dancing merrily.

Walt Disney's
LADY

Once there was a beautiful cocker spaniel named Lady. She had long, silky ears and a very ladylike bark. She lived in an elegant house with her human family, Jim Dear and Darling. She loved them very much, and they loved her, too.

Jim Dear and Darling gave Lady just about everything a dog could want. They set up a cozy bed for her. They brought her plenty of bones. They even used a fancy dish for her supper.

Jim Dear and Darling often took Lady to have her fur and nails trimmed. Lady liked to watch in the mirror as the shopkeeper clipped and combed her coat.

On warm afternoons, Lady went for rides in a horse-drawn carriage with Jim Dear and Darling. Many of the neighborhood dogs admired how pretty she looked in the coach, including Lady's friends Jock, a Scottish terrier, and Trusty, a bloodhound.

One day, Jock and Trusty came to visit Lady in her backyard.

"Jim Dear and Darling have done so much for me," Lady told her friends. "I wish I could do more for them, but what can a little dog do?"

Trusty had an idea. "You could carry things for them," he suggested.

"And bring things to them," Jock added brightly.

So Lady learned to catch the newspaper that the paperboy tossed into the yard each morning. Then she brought it to Jim Dear in the kitchen.

Sometimes the paper would tear as Lady squeezed it through her doggie door, but Jim Dear never minded. He always patted her on the head and exclaimed, "Good Lady! Good dog!"

Lady was very pleased.

Soon a baby boy came to live with Lady and her family. Almost overnight, everything seemed to change. Jim Dear and Darling were always busy taking care of the baby. They didn't pay much attention to Lady anymore. One summer day, they even forgot to give Lady her bath.

Later that morning, Lady asked Jock and Trusty why her family was acting so strangely.

Just then, a mutt named Tramp happened to pass by. He was a stray from a much rougher part of town. He answered Lady from the edge of her yard.

"Babies will scratch you and pinch you and even pull your ears," Tramp said. "But worst of all, once a baby moves in, your family will forget all about you—"

"Look here, laddie, who are you to butt in?" Jock cut him off.

"The voice of experience, buster," Tramp said.

Tramp sighed. "Having a family is just too much trouble for a dog," he said.

"Don't you have a family?" Lady asked.

"Lots," Tramp replied. "I stop by a different house every night for a home-cooked meal, but then I leave to go back to the streets where I'm free."

Just then, Jock and Trusty were called home for dinner. They left, but no one had called Lady. She felt more alone than ever.

Tramp smiled at her. "Something tells me it's suppertime. Come on," he said. "I'll show you what I mean."

That evening, Lady did all sorts of new and exciting things. First, Tramp showed her how to jump fences. Then he suggested they chase a cat.

"But we shouldn't," Lady told him.

"I know. That's what makes it fun," Tramp said.

But Lady just stood there. She was puzzled.

"Ah, come on, kid," Tramp said.

"We won't hurt the cat, will we?" she asked.

"Hurt him? No," Tramp promised. "We'll just stir him up a bit."

And that's just what they did.

Later that night, Tramp took Lady to his favorite Italian restaurant, Tony's. Lady ate spaghetti and meatballs for the first time.

After dinner, they went for a walk in the park. As they sat on a hilltop overlooking the village, Tramp said, "Look down there. Tell me what you see."

"Well, I see nice homes with yards and fences," Lady said.

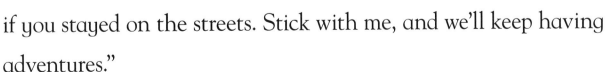

"Exactly. You're all cooped up when you have a human family," Tramp said. "But you could be free if you stayed on the streets. Stick with me, and we'll keep having adventures."

Lady didn't answer. She wasn't sure what she wanted.

The two dogs decided to go back into town. They hopped over fences, crawled under gates, and took shortcuts through people's yards. After a while, Lady's paws began to hurt. Tramp suggested they stop to rest in an alley.

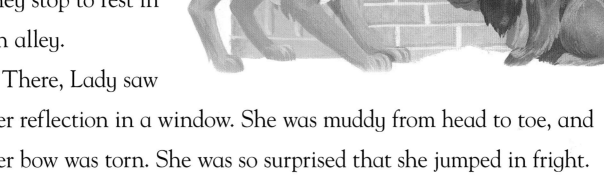

There, Lady saw her reflection in a window. She was muddy from head to toe, and her bow was torn. She was so surprised that she jumped in fright. Then she hid her face in her paws.

"Oh!" she cried. "I'm not a lady. I'm just an ugly little dog with muddy fur and a dirty, torn ribbon. I *hate* looking like this. Take me home, Tramp, please."

Tramp nodded. "Come on, I'll take you home."

Tramp knew a shortcut back to Lady's house. When they arrived, Jim Dear was on the porch. Lady ran up the stairs.

"Lady!" cried Jim Dear. He hugged her. "Why did you run away? We were so worried about you!"

Lady barked happily.

Tramp stood at the foot of the stairs. He wagged his tail and barked, too. He was very polite.

"Well," said Jim Dear in a friendly voice. "Come here, boy."

He patted Tramp and smiled at Lady.

"Bring in your friend, Lady," said Jim Dear. "I think we can use two dogs around here to help with the baby, don't you agree?"

From then on, life was better than ever. Jim Dear and Darling were happy to have Lady back at home. And they were especially pleased to have two dogs to look after their baby.

It turned out, Tramp liked having a real home with a real family. He didn't even mind bath days . . . too much.

But Lady was probably the happiest of all. She knew that Jim Dear and Darling loved her, and she was glad to have Tramp by her side.

Walt Disney's
Old Yeller

Nobody knew where Old Yeller came from. He just turned up one day at the Coateses' cabin, sniffing and snuffing and wagging his tail.

The Coates boys, Arliss and Travis, looked him over. Not that he was much to look at. He was big and clumsy and yellow.

But Old Yeller was full of tricks, too. Whenever anyone picked up a stick or a stone, Old Yeller threw himself on the ground. He rolled around, howling and yowling worse than a wildcat.

Old Yeller and Arliss took to each other right away. "He's my dog now!" Arliss said. "He's mine! Isn't he, Mama?"

But Mrs. Coates wasn't sure they should keep the dog.

"If your papa was here, he'd know what to do," she said.

But Mr. Coates was far away, selling their cows. He wouldn't be back for months. So Mrs. Coates told Arliss that Old Yeller could stay—for now.

Whooping and hollering, Arliss ran for the pond with Old Yeller right behind him. When he was standing still, Old Yeller looked as though he couldn't walk without tripping over his own feet. But when he started running, he was like a streak of lightning greased with hot bear oil. He was swift and sure and a sight to see!

In fact, Old Yeller was so fast that he once caught a good-sized catfish in the pond for Arliss. Another time he helped Travis drive some thieving raccoons out of the corn patch. And he was a wonder at herding cows and hogs.

Then one day, Arliss did something he shouldn't have and got himself into real trouble. He caught a bear cub by the leg. And worse, he didn't let go, even when the cub's mother charged at him, snarling and growling.

Suddenly, Old Yeller came bounding up. He tore right into that old bear.

While Old Yeller fought the bear, Mrs. Coates and Travis pulled Arliss away from the cub.

Soon the big bear had enough of the fighting and ran off
through the brush with her cub.

When he saw that Arliss was safe, Old Yeller wagged his tail.

"Oh, you crazy,
wonderful old
dog!" Mrs.
Coates said.
She knew
then that she
was right to let
Arliss keep
Old Yeller.

A few days later, a man rode up to the cabin. His name was Mr. Sanderson, and he had lost a dog—a big yellow one that was full of tricks. Old Yeller was *his* dog.

When Mr. Sanderson started to take Old Yeller away, Arliss shouted, "You can't have my dog!"

Mr. Sanderson looked at Arliss and then got down from his horse.

"Just a minute, young fellow," he said. "What's that in your pocket?"

"A horned toad," Arliss said, and held it out.

"Finest horned toad I ever saw," Mr. Sanderson said. Right then and there, Mr. Sanderson offered to swap his dog for Arliss's toad . . . if Mrs. Coates threw in a good home-cooked meal.

Mrs. Coates smiled and nodded.

And so Mr. Sanderson got a toad and a meal, and Arliss got Old Yeller.

"You're really my dog now, aren't you, boy?" Arliss said.

Old Yeller just wagged his tail and lay down in front of the fire. He knew he was there to stay.

Walt Disney's
Sleeping Beauty

Once upon a time, in a faraway land, a princess was born. The happy king and queen named their daughter Aurora. They invited everyone in the kingdom to the palace to celebrate her birth— everyone except the evil fairy Maleficent.

Angry, the wicked fairy arrived at the party and put a curse on the princess.

"Before the sun sets on her sixteenth birthday," Maleficent promised, "she shall prick her finger on the spindle of a spinning wheel . . . and die!"

Then, in a burst of green smoke, the evil fairy disappeared.

Fortunately, the
three good fairies,
Flora, Fauna, and
Merryweather,
were there, too. As
soon as Maleficent

vanished, they tried to soften the curse.

"Sweet princess," declared Merryweather, "not in death but just
in sleep, the fateful prophecy you'll keep. And from this slumber
you shall wake, when True Love's Kiss the spell shall break."

Then, disguised as peasant women, the fairies brought the baby
to a cottage in the woods, where they would raise her and keep her
identity a secret until the night of her sixteenth birthday.

The years passed, and
the princess grew into
a sweet and lovely girl
known as Briar Rose.
Although Briar
Rose's only friends were
the forest animals, she
dreamed of falling
in love.

Then, on the day of her sixteenth birthday, the princess's dream
came true. A prince named Phillip was riding through the woods
and saw Briar Rose dancing with her animal friends. He stepped up
and asked her to dance with him instead.

Briar Rose had been taught not to talk to strangers, but for some
reason she trusted this prince. And so she agreed to the dance.

Soon the two were falling in love.

Meanwhile, back in their cottage, the three good fairies tried to plan a birthday surprise for Briar Rose—without using magic.

Fauna tried to whip up a fancy cake, while Flora and Merryweather tried to sew an elegant dress. But the cake was a disaster, and the dress looked terrible.

Merryweather decided to get the fairies' wands.

Using their magic, the fairies quickly finished their preparations. But as they used their wands, colorful sparks came out of the chimney. Maleficent's crow saw them and flew off to tell the evil fairy that he had found the princess.

When Briar Rose arrived back at the cottage, she told the fairies about the handsome stranger she'd met. The good fairies knew it was time to tell Briar Rose the truth: her real name was Princess Aurora, and she would be returning to the castle that evening.

Aurora followed the fairies to the palace, where the king and queen eagerly awaited her. Although the princess was excited to see her parents, she was sad because she didn't think she'd ever get to see the handsome stranger again.

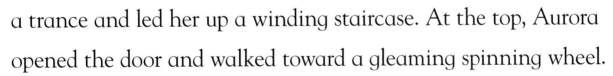

At the palace, the fairies took Aurora upstairs. But when they left the girl alone, Maleficent appeared.

She put the princess in a trance and led her up a winding staircase. At the top, Aurora opened the door and walked toward a gleaming spinning wheel.

"Touch the spindle! Touch it, I say!" Maleficent ordered.

The princess obeyed. She pricked her finger and fell to the floor. And that is where the good fairies found her.

Flora, Fauna, and Merryweather couldn't bear to break the king's heart with the news of Aurora's fate. So they put everyone in the castle to sleep until the spell could be broken. Then the fairies flew off to find the boy from the forest. Only his kiss could wake the princess.

When the good fairies told Prince Phillip what had happened, he raced toward the castle. But Maleficent was not about to let him rescue the princess. She used her magic to turn herself into an enormous fire-breathing dragon.

Using all his strength, Prince Phillip aimed his sword at the dragon's heart. With one mighty blow, the dragon was no more.

Prince Phillip raced through the castle to the room where the princess slept. He knelt by Aurora's side and gently kissed her.

Slowly, Aurora's eyes opened. She smiled when she saw the handsome stranger from the forest. He was her one true love.

Aurora sat up and took Prince Phillip's hand. And from that moment on, the two lived happily ever after.

Walt Disney's
MANNI
the Donkey

Manni the donkey was exploring his new farm home. He sniffed the bright summer air. Then he brayed—a big, noisy bray that woke all the other animals.

Suddenly, Manni noticed a patch of green beyond the garden gate. It was the forest!

Raising his long, pointed ears, Manni brayed again, so loudly that the straw in the haystack shook with the sound. Then he trotted over to the gate and opened it with his hoof.

In the forest, Manni met Perri, a little red squirrel.

"Who are you? Can you climb trees?" Perri chattered.

"I'm Manni," the donkey said. "I can't climb at all. I just want to see the forest."

But before Manni could ask Perri any questions about the forest, she had disappeared.

Next two baby deer and their mother darted from the bushes.

"Who are you?" the mother deer asked.

"I'm Manni. I want to see the forest," Manni answered. "And I'd like to be your friend."

But the mother deer did not trust Manni, and she and her fawns plunged back into the bushes.

Next three rabbits hopped from the underbrush. But when they saw Manni, they ran away, too. This continued for some time. Every animal who saw Manni was afraid.

Finally, he met a pheasant. "I don't believe you belong here," the bird said. "What does Tambo think?"

"Who is Tambo?" asked Manni.

"Tambo is King of the Forest," the pheasant answered. "He wears a crown of horns and eats only grass and leaves."

"I eat grass, too," said Manni. "I will find Tambo and we will be friends."

247

But when Manni found Tambo, he was not friendly at all. In fact, he lowered his horns to attack.

"I'm Manni," the donkey said, trying to be brave. "I'd like to be your friend."

But Tambo just snorted. "I don't like you one bit," he said. "You're noisy and you're different. I don't think you belong in the forest at all. Now, be off!"

Manni's ears drooped. His eyes were sad. Maybe he *should* go back to the farm.

Manni looked for the path home. But every path looked alike. He was lost!

Suddenly, Perri darted between Manni's legs.

Before Manni could ask if the squirrel knew the way home, he heard snapping twigs. A sharp, foxy smell came to Manni's nose, and a red fox crashed through the underbrush. It was after Perri!

Manni raised his ears, opened his mouth, and brayed. The sound was as loud as thunder in the quiet woods.

Scared, the fox whirled around, tucked his tail between his legs, and ran.

Just then, Tambo crashed through the bushes. "You saved Perri's life," he said. "You are welcome to stay in the forest."

"Thank you," Manni replied. "The forest is wonderful, but I don't really belong here. Will someone please show me the way home?"

And so, as the moon rose, that is just what Manni's new friends did.

Walt Disney's
DONALD DUCK'S TOY SAILBOAT

"There!" said Donald Duck. "At last it's done!"

Donald stood back to look at his toy sailboat. Making it had been a big job. It had taken him all summer. But now the boat was finished. And it was beautiful!

"Building sailboats is hungry work," Donald said to himself. So he fixed himself a fine lunch.

"Now to try out the boat on the lake," he said. But Donald's hard work had made him sleepy, so he settled down for a nap. He would try out the boat later.

Outside Donald's cottage, in the old elm tree, there lived two little chipmunks, Chip and Dale. And they had had no lunch at all.

"I'm hungry," said Chip, rubbing his empty stomach.

"Me too," said little Dale. Then suddenly, he shouted, "Look!"

Chip looked and looked. At last he spied it—one lone acorn still clinging to the bough of an old oak tree beside the lake.

Down the elm tree the chipmunks raced, across to the oak, and up its rough-barked trunk.

"Mine!" cried Chip, reaching for the nut.

"I saw it first!" Dale cried.

257

The two little
chipmunks pushed
and they tugged and
they tussled until the
acorn slipped through
their fingers and
fell—*kerplunk*—into
the lake.

Chip and Dale
watched sadly as
the acorn floated
away. Then Dale
saw something else. On a little island out in the middle of the lake
stood a great big oak tree weighed down with acorns on every side.

As Chip wondered how they could reach the island, Dale spied a
way across the water.

On the mantel in Donald Duck's cottage was his toy sailboat. It would be perfect for reaching the little island!

"Come on," said Dale. So away the two chipmunks raced, straight up to the door and into the cottage.

Chip and Dale had the sailboat down and almost out the door when Donald stirred in his sleep.

"Nice day for a sail," he said dreamily, as the boat slipped smoothly past him.

261

Soon after, Donald woke up completely.

"Now to try out my boat," he said.

Suddenly, something outside the window caught his eye. It was his sailboat, out on the lake!

"I'll fix those chipmunks!" Donald said.

He pulled out his fishing rod and reel and chose a painted fly. It looked just like a nut.

"This will do," Donald grinned.

Donald cast his line into the water. It landed with a *plop* beside the toy boat.

"Look! Look at this!" cried Dale. He leaned over the edge of the boat to pull in the floating fly.

"A nut!" said Chip. "We'll toss it in the hold and have it for dinner tonight."

As soon as the nut was in the hold, Donald pulled in the line. But Chip and Dale realized that something was wrong. They pulled the nut out of the hold and flung it at Donald. Soon he was tangled in his own fishing line.

While Donald tried to tug himself free, the chipmunks set sail once more. Soon they reached the little island. Chip and Dale danced along the oak tree's branches, knocking hundreds of acorns to the ground. Then they hauled their harvest on board.

Meanwhile, free at last, Donald jumped into his canoe and raced after the chipmunks. Donald laughed as he saw the chipmunks loading up the boat. "Oh, well," he said. "At least I know the sailboat really will sail. Now let's see what those little fellows do."

And can you guess what the chipmunks did? They stored their nuts in a hollow tree. And they took Donald's toy sailboat back, and put it right where it belonged!

Walt Disney's
The Jungle Book

Many strange legends are told of the jungles of far-off India. They speak of Bagheera the black panther, and of Baloo the bear. They tell of Kaa the sly python, and of the lord of the jungle, the great tiger Shere Khan. But of all these legends, none is so strange as the story of a small boy named Mowgli.

Mowgli, you see, had been left all alone in the jungle as a baby. He was found by Bagheera the panther. But Bagheera could not give the small, helpless Man-cub care and nourishment, and so he took the boy to live with a wolf family with young cubs of their own.

Ten times the rains came and went, and still Mowgli lived with the wolves. Then, one day, everything changed. The tiger, Shere Khan, returned to the jungle.

Akela, the leader of the pack, gathered the wolves at Council Rock.

"The Man-cub can no longer stay with the pack," he said. "The strength of the pack is no match for the tiger."

"Perhaps I can be of help," said Bagheera. "I know a Man-village where he'll be safe."

And so it was decided. Bagheera would take the Man-cub to safety.

When the greenish light of the jungle morning slipped through the leaves, Bagheera and Mowgli set out. But Mowgli did not wish to leave the jungle. And so, as Bagheera slept that night, the Man-cub slipped down a length of trailing vine and ran away.

Mowgli had not gone far when he saw a baby elephant march past him. Mowgli decided that he wanted to be an elephant, too. And so he fell in line behind the baby.

But when Colonel Hathi, the proud leader of the elephant herd, found Mowgli, he was very angry.

"A Man-cub. Oh, this is treason. Sabotage!" Hathi cried. "I'll have no Man-cub in my jungle!"

Mowgli ran away from the elephants . . . and straight into a big gray bear named Baloo. Soon the two were playing together. There were coconuts to crack, bananas to peel, and sweet, juicy pawpaws to pick from jungle trees. Mowgli had never had so much fun!

"You're gonna make one swell bear!" Baloo told Mowgli as the two romped through the jungle together. "Just you wait and see."

Baloo and Mowgli were enjoying a dip in a jungle river when down swooped the monkey folk. Before Baloo knew what was happening, the monkeys had snatched up the Man-cub. They tossed him through the air from hand to hand and swung away with him through the trees.

Off in the jungle, Bagheera heard
Mowgli's cry.

"What happened to Mowgli?"
Bagheera asked Baloo.

"Them monkeys carried him off!"
gasped Baloo.

Bagheera and Baloo raced to the
ruined city where the monkeys made their
home. They found Mowgli a prisoner of
King Louie, the king of the apes.

"What I desire is Man's red fire," King
Louie told Mowgli. "Now give me the
secret so I can be like you."

But before Mowgli could answer,
Baloo and Bagheera whisked
him away.

"Look, Mowgli," Baloo said when they were safe. "I got to take you back to the Man-village."

"But you said we were partners," Mowgli said.

Baloo tried to explain, but Mowgli would not listen. Angry, he ran away into the jungle, all alone. And that is where he was when Shere Khan found him at last.

When Mowgli caught
sight of the tiger, Shere Khan
asked, "Well, Man-cub, aren't you
going to run?"

But Mowgli did not have the
wisdom to be afraid. "Why should
I run?" he asked, staring
at Shere Khan as
the tiger gathered
himself to pounce.
"You don't scare me."

With a mighty roar,
Shere Khan lunged at Mowgli.
He would teach the boy to be afraid of him.

Suddenly, there was a flash of lightning. A
dead tree nearby caught fire.

Mowgli snatched a burning branch and tied it to Shere Khan's tail. Terrified, the tiger ran away.

Mowgli was very pleased with himself. But he had also realized that perhaps the jungle *was* a dangerous place for him. It was time to go to the Man-village with Bagheera and Baloo.

The next morning, Mowgli, Baloo, and Bagheera reached the Man-village. Through the bushes, Mowgli heard a sound he did not know. It was the song of a village girl who had come to the river to fill her water jug.

As he listened to her song, Mowgli felt that he must follow the girl. He crept up the path to the village, drawn by the girl and her song.

Baloo and Bagheera watched the boy's small figure as long as it could be seen. When Mowgli vanished inside the village gate, Bagheera sighed a deep sigh. He would miss his friend.

Then, with one last look behind them, Baloo and Bagheera headed back into the jungle.

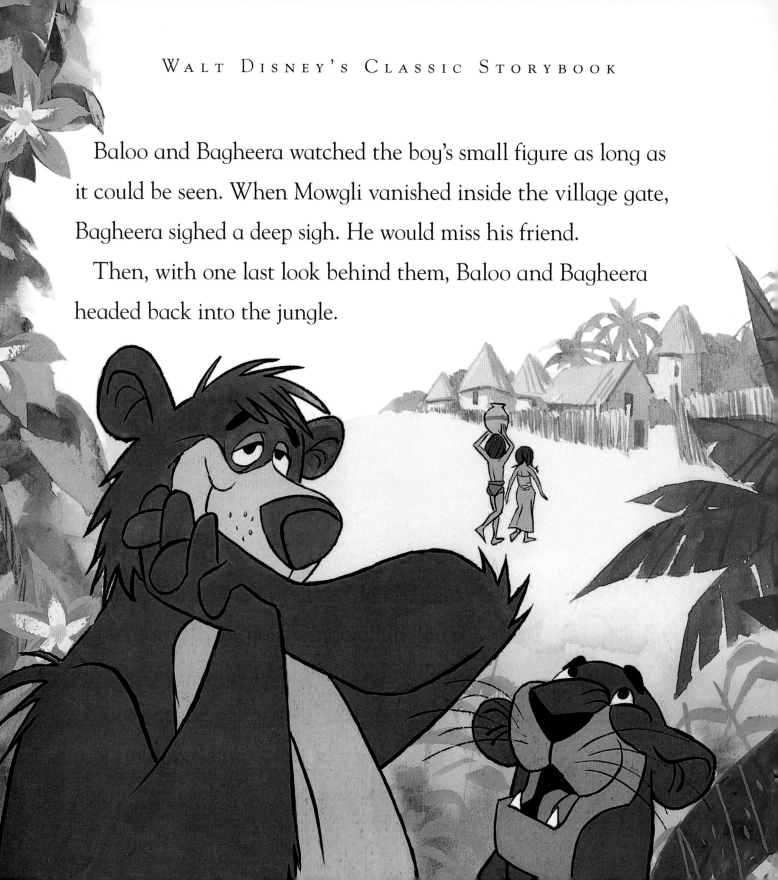

Walt Disney's
Herbie
the Love Bug

Each morning when Herbie took Bill Botts to work, the Love Bug greeted his friends with a cheery beep. There were cars and trucks of every size . . . buses . . . cabs . . . hot-dog carts . . . bulldozers and steam shovels.

Herbie liked them all. It was nice to have so many friends.

One afternoon, Bill and Herbie came home to find that a pretty new neighbor had moved in next door.

Herbie honked and winked his lights. But he wasn't looking at the young lady. He was looking at her pretty yellow car.

The young lady thought Bill was honking at her and hurried inside.

"Did you have to do that, Herbie?" Bill groaned. "Now I'll never get to meet her."

All evening, Bill thought about his new neighbor. He promised himself that he would apologize to her for the way Herbie had behaved.

On the way to work the next morning, Bill stopped beside the young lady at a red light. When Herbie saw her car, his hood popped up and his engine raced. Embarrassed, Bill blushed until he was as red as the stoplight itself.

After that, Herbie couldn't think of anything but the yellow car. He even forgot to watch where he was going.

"Herbie!" Bill shouted on the way to work. "You're going the wrong way!"

"Herbie!" he screamed on the way home. "Watch out for that steamroller!"

A week passed, and Herbie acted worse each day. Then, one evening, Bill discovered the young lady sitting on her front step.

"You look upset," he said. "My name is Bill. Can I help?"

"I'm Ann Peterson," she answered. "Someone has stolen my car!"

"How terrible!" Bill cried. "We'd better report this right away!"

Herbie opened a door for Miss Peterson and rushed away down the street. In no time, they had arrived at the police station.

Herbie tried to wait, but he just couldn't. His little yellow friend needed his help! While Bill and Ann went into the station, Herbie zoomed off to find the yellow car.

Up one street and down the next Herbie flew. The city was full of cars—new ones, old ones, shiny ones, dull ones. But Herbie didn't see that very special yellow car anywhere.

Soon Bill and Ann came out of the police station.

"Look!" she cried. "Herbie's gone!"

"Oh, no!" Bill moaned. "Now we have *two* missing cars to look for."

Meanwhile, Herbie sped across the city. He had to find the little yellow car.

Finally, he spotted her. She was speeding in the other direction.

Herbie spun around and streaked after his little friend. The chase was on!

Faster and faster the two cars went. Herbie began beeping at his friends as he zoomed by. Soon, they had joined the chase, too.

The thief suddenly found his way blocked by dozens of cars, all with their lights flashing. He was trapped!

Herbie's friends opened a path, and Herbie zipped through, just as the man leaped out of the yellow car and tried to run away.

The Love Bug snapped his hood and caught the man by the seat of his pants. He was still holding him when a police car arrived with its siren wailing.

Out jumped two policemen—with Bill and Ann.

"Herbie!" Bill shouted. "You're all right!"

"And he's rescued my car!" Ann cried. "How can I ever thank you?"

"I don't know," Bill said with a grin, "but how about a picnic while we talk about it?"

That evening, Bill and Ann sat quietly on a blanket and watched the sun set over the ocean. Meanwhile, Herbie frolicked in the water.

"Herbie's certainly happy tonight," Ann said. "I'm glad. I'm very proud of him."

"So am I," said Bill. And he winked at the little yellow car, who looked as if she was very proud of Herbie, too.